I0646860

MISHTI THE MIRZAPURI LABRADOR

# MISHTI

## THE MIRZAPURI LABRADOR

### Urf Mishti ke Karname

## GILLIAN WRIGHT

### Illustrated by Anitha Balachandran

SPEAKING
**TIGER**

SPEAKING TIGER PUBLISHING PVT. LTD
4381/4 Ansari Road, Daryaganj,
New Delhi–110002, India

Copyright © Gillian Wright 2017
Illustrations Copyright © Anitha Balachandran 2017

ISBN: 978-93-86338-65-5
eISBN: 978-93-86338-64-8

10 9 8 7 6 5 4 3 2 1

Typeset in Goudy Old Style by SÜRYA, New Delhi
Printed at Gopsons Papers Ltd

All rights reserved.
No part of this publication may be reproduced,
transmitted, or stored in a retrieval system, in any form or
by any means, electronic, mechanical, photocopying,
recording or otherwise, without the prior
permission of the publisher.

This book is sold subject to the condition that it shall not, by way of trade
or otherwise, be lent, resold, hired out, or otherwise circulated, without
the publisher's prior consent, in any form of binding or cover other than
that in which it is published.

# CONTENTS

# MISHTI FINDS A HOME

Mishti was born in the town of Mirzapur on the banks of the Ganga, where the great river takes a sharp turn on her way down to the holy city of Benares. Mishti didn't know she was born there, she just knew the warmth of her mother and the taste of milk. After two weeks, little golden, mewing Mishti opened her puppy eyes and saw her mother. Two weeks later, two hands came down and took her away.

These two hands belonged to Sally. Sally too had been born in Mirzapur and lived in her parents' old house, the burra bungalow, next to the river in the quiet end of town. She cuddled Mishti as they drove there and Mishti looked up at her and out of the window at her first sight of the world outside. Her eyes were bright. Adventure was in her blood.

The car drove through the gates of the compound and came to a halt. Sally carried Mishti past the grapefruit and mango trees, and vegetable patches where hathi-chak and other mysterious vegetables were grown. She put her down on the lawn. Mishti smelt the grass. Clouds of butterflies fluttered between the bushes. Mishti tried to catch them.

The burra bungalow was big and old, with a verandah all the way round, and, Mishti discovered, chewy cane furniture. Mishti lapped up a milky meal in the kitchen and explored indoors where the floors were covered with beautiful, antique brown and golden carpets made by hand by the mastercraftsmen of Mirzapur. This bungalow was now Mishti's home and she slept snuggled up against Sally in a high bed.

She soon discovered she was not the only Labrador in the compound. There was also a large, light-eyed golden Labrador, full of confidence, and his name was Sultan. He was Mishti's father and best friend of Edward, Sally's brother.

Edward was not fond of walking. So, twice a day Sultan would walk with Sulaiman Chacha—who was the the oldest man on the compound, and the best at looking after dogs—all the way around the compound and meet all the gardeners and staff. There were a lot of staff as the compound was the headquarters of the biggest carpet company in the whole of Mirzapur. Every evening after his dinner, Sultan would come and meet Sally and Edward and their guests on the verandah. He was expert at eating pistachio nuts and spitting out the shells. Few Labradors know how to do this.

Two of the people who watched in disbelief as Sultan spat out a pistachio shell, were Mark and Gilly. They lived in Delhi and were old friends of Edward and Sally. They found tiny Mishti enchanting. Their Labrador had just died, and Edward was sad for them. He suggested they might like to take Mishti. But Mark and Gilly were not ready to have another dog. Before they left, Edward called all the staff of the burra bungalow, and all the children who lived on the compound, for a photograph with the visitors from

Delhi. Sultan and Mishti were naturally included. He sent a copy of the photograph to Mark and Gilly to remember them by.

# MISHTI AND SULTAN

Mishti loved Sultan and Sultan loved her. As she grew bigger she played around his feet and teased him, jumping on him and racing after him as he went for his morning and evening tours of the compound. She found them great fun. But Sally noticed that something was wrong. Mishti had a limp. Her legs didn't look quite right. Sally and Edward had a talk. The next thing Mishti knew, she was being put on the floor of an Ambassador car and driven for many, many hours down bumpy roads to the great city of Kolkata. Kolkata smelt of cars and smoke, but Edward knew a vet there, and the vet said Mishti had to stay in Kolkata and have all the right kinds of food and medicine to get her legs right. For the first time Mishti missed her home, but being a true Labrador she ate everything the vet gave her, and her legs became stronger. Then one day she was put back on the floor of another Ambassador and driven for many, many bumpy hours until she reached Mirzapur.

The compound gates opened. The car door opened. Mishti jumped out and ran into Sally's arms, then jumped down, greeted Sulaiman, and ran round and round Sultan and licked his face. She was so happy to be home. She chased the butterflies and barked a joyful bark. Sultan was very happy to have his daughter back. He didn't understand why she had been taken away, but he did understand that he didn't want her to be taken away ever again. He was going to protect her. And so he began to regard visitors with suspicion. Were they coming to take Mishti away?

Now if you run a carpet company, a lot of people come to see you. There are all the people who work there, like the people in the office, and the carpet designers, and the weavers, and the dyers, and the boilermen, and the carpet finishers, and the families of all of these, as well as the guests—particularly people who want to buy carpets. These last ones are important because you need people to buy carpets if you are in the carpet business. Sultan watched them all suspiciously.

One day three buyers came. They were standing near Mishti and Sultan decided that they looked just the kind of people who would want to take her away. So he walked towards them in a determined sort of way. He glared at them. The hairs on his back rose. They began to look nervous. Then he leaped towards them barking and snarling, with his teeth bared. The buyers were terrified and ran towards the compound wall. Sultan ran after them and kept them there, pinned against the wall for a good ten minutes before Sulaiman Chacha came, poured water over him and pulled him away. Sultan, however, was unrepentant, and this became his favourite way of greeting strangers.

Edward was not pleased. His buyers were complaining. The company would suffer. And so he decided to send both Sultan and Mishti away. They

were found different homes, both in Mirzapur, and the big compound gates closed against them. But the staff of the compound missed them, and so did Sally, and Edward missed them too. He thought that the problem started because Sultan was protecting Mishti, so if Sultan came back alone, then perhaps things would be all right. So after a few months, he brought Sultan back home, and Sultan began to live peacefully again, walking round the compound twice a day in the company of Sulaiman Chacha. Without Mishti he had no reason to attack strangers.

Mishti was now living with a doctor in Mirzapur, but her adventures were about to begin.

# MISHTI ON THE MOVE

Part of Edward's job was to travel to places to look after the business of selling Mirzapur's beautiful carpets around the world. One day when he was in Delhi, he went to meet Mark and Gilly.

They asked about Sultan and his daughter, and Edward said, 'What a pity that you couldn't take Mishti.'

Gilly and Mark looked at each other and said, 'Perhaps we could now.'

Whenever Edward needed something done, he called on the person who organized his life, knew him best and was the only person who could get him to keep to his diabetic diet and take his medicine on time. Now too he called out, 'Bhagwan Das!'

Bhagwan Das was practical and intelligent, and could solve any problem. He came into the room from the kitchen, where he was supervising preparations for dinner. The matter of Mishti was for him an easy one to solve. He dialled a number on his mobile, and gave a few instructions, 'Doctor Sahib ke ghar se Mishti ko compound le aana hai, nehlana hai aur Dilli ko le aana hai.' He told Edward that all was done. Gilly and Mark looked on in amazement, and wondered if they were doing the right thing. A dog is a big responsibility.

After dinner, Edward and Bhagwan Das left, and Gilly and Mark were left to prepare for their new visitor. The weather was cool, so Mishti would need some bedding, and she would also need a water and a food bowl. Mirzapur was a long way from Delhi, over 800 kilometres to the east. They waited for the whole of the next day but Mishti did not arrive. They went to bed, and were in deep sleep when suddenly at three a.m. the doorbell rang. Gilly climbed out of bed and tiptoed down the long dark hall. She reached the door and opened the latch.

As soon as the door opened a crack, Mishti's nose appeared and then Mishti, pushing her way in—small and gold, straining on her lead with all her might. Behind her came a team of Mirzapuris. Mishti walked right past Gilly and right past Mark and across their flat straight to the water bowl, as if she already knew where it would be. Having lapped up a great deal of water, she pricked up her ears and looked around. The men who came with her were handing over her blanket, and a bottle of massage oil for her legs (she still tended to limp). Then they said goodbye and left.

Now there was just Gilly, Mark and Mishti. Gilly took the dog-bed she had bought and which looked far too big for this very small Labrador and Mishti's blanket, and laid them on the floor in the bedroom. Mishti sniffed around, and pattered in and out. Eventually she too went to sleep. As if she knew she had come home.

# MISHTI MAKES HER MARK

The next morning, Mark and Gilly took a proper look at their new puppy. Her face was like a golden upside-down triangle and her ears flopped forwards like two little upside-down triangles. She had silky smooth fur and neat little paws. Her eyes were shining, bright and black, and seemed lined with kajal. She looked alert, full of mischief and a little wild. And she was enormously bouncy.

As she was already ten months old, one great puppy problem was solved. She already knew not to do susu and potty in the house. But she still had a lot to learn, and Mark and Gilly had a lot to learn about her. First of all, they let her out to run around the garden. Then they took her for an experimental short walk around the block.

After breakfast Mishti explored her new home. It was much smaller than the big spaces of Mirzapur. But like the burra bungalow it was part home, part office. Visitors would drop in, not to buy carpets, but to discuss important things like the Future of India. Some came on her first day. Gilly invited them to sit down and have some tea. Mishti meanwhile decided to give them her special welcome. She hopped in the air to make her barks as loud as possible, and then sped towards them, her tail sweeping from side to side and knocking various pieces of bric-a-brac off the tables by the sofa. Gilly swooped down to move the teacups out of her reach just in time. The guests were the sort that didn't like dogs. One of them screamed, but Gilly pulled Mishti away before she licked her, and managed to persuade her that she was only a friendly puppy. Mishti lay down and watched intently as they began their discussions.

After a few moments she stood up, her eyes

gleaming. She curled her head round towards her tail. She tried hard to get her nose to touch her bottom but couldn't quite manage it, so she started to spin round to get closer. Then she started to spin faster. And faster. Soon she was a blur. The guests couldn't keep their attention on the Future of India, and stared at her. Gilly leapt up and held Mishti still, patting her and apologizing.

As soon as Gilly let her go, Mishti again curled her head round towards her tail. She still couldn't quite reach her bottom and before you could say 'Dog biscuits!' she was whirling around at 100 kilometres an hour, chasing her tail.

Every time Gilly stopped her, she started again, and kept on doing it. It was a strange kind of entertainment. Gilly had heard of whirling dervishes, but a whirling Labrador?

For some reason the visitors didn't stay long, and once they had left Gilly consulted the vet.

He explained that Mishti chased her tail because she had an itchy bottom and she had an itchy bottom because she had stomach worms. All dogs get worms and it is very important to give them de-worming medicine regularly. The vet prescribed extra doses of de-worming medicine to make sure all the worms were dealt with.

While the itchiness was subsiding, Mark and Gilly thought it would be a good idea to get her to do something else besides chase her tail. They had loved playing catch with their old Labrador, and so they decided to play catch with Mishti. Gilly gently threw her a soft rubber ball. Mishti didn't move a muscle and the ball bounced off her nose. Gilly tried again. This time too it bounced off her nose. Obviously no one in Mirzapur had taught Mishti how to catch!

The question was how to teach her. Gilly and Mark started playing catch with one another, and were pleased to see that Mishti paid close attention. 'Come on, Mishti!' said Gilly. Mishti ran over and stood between them as if she was playing piggy-in-the-middle. Gilly threw the ball quite low, and Mishti leapt up and caught it. Gilly and Mark clapped and cheered and gave her a cuddle. She realized she had done good.

Now there was no stopping her. She not only began catching, she brought things back, which is exactly what a Labrador is bred to do. Their full name is Labrador Retriever and they are meant to find things and fetch them. Now every time she was thrown a ball or toy, Mishti would catch it, or run after it and bring it back, although often she held on to it tightly in her teeth until Gilly prised her jaws apart and said 'Drop!' Mishti never got tired of playing. As an experiment, Gilly sat on the bed holding her squeaky green rubber hedgehog. Three hundred times she threw the hedgehog and three hundred times Mishti climbed on the bed and gave it back. Suddenly Gilly realized that Mishti had a lot in common with some children she knew.

Nunu, Mana and Tush were sisters. While Mishti was happy catching a squeaky hedgehog three hundred times, the sisters were happy to spend the whole day playing on the slide outside the local McDonalds. This they liked to do whenever they came to stay, as they often did.

When the girls and Mishti met, they immediately became firm friends. Mishti deserted Mark and Gilly and instead slept in the spare bedroom with them. They in turn adored her and trained her to 'Sit and Stay'. With a bit of dog snack in their hands (a dog snack being anything edible except for onions, chillies or tomatoes), they would say 'Baith' or 'Sit' with a lot of emphasis on the T. Mishti would sit and fix her eyes on them. Then they would raise their forefinger and say 'Stay', and would walk away. When they thought Mishti had 'stayed' enough, they would call her and

throw her the treat. This game kept them all happy for hours, especially when it was interrupted with breaks for catch and football.

Mishti's idea of a game of football was not the same as a human's. She had no inclination to kick the ball. But she loved to run after a football and try to grab hold of it with her mouth. However, Mishti was a small Labrador, with a small mouth and a football is big. So there was no way she could get her mouth round it, and the ball kept slipping out between her legs and getting away. This looked very funny.

One day, Nunu came with a brand new football her father had bought from a roadside stall for a whole hundred rupees. The new toy was a special attraction for Mishti. New toys were new fun. The girls laughed and laughed as Mishti chased the ball and tried and failed to pick it up in her mouth. Then with one super-doggy effort, Mishti managed to get a hold in the stitching of the ball and her canine tooth pierced it. The ball became a little flabbier. Mishti tried harder, she fixed her teeth in it and thrashed it around as if she wanted to beat the life out of it. 'Aiayeeee!' screamed Nunu, bursting into tears, 'Phaar diya!'

Indeed she had punctured it. While Nunu cried, her sisters laughed, and Mishti ran up and down with the ball, which to her mind, was much better now she could get her teeth into it. By the end of the afternoon it was more like a pancake than a football. Nunu gave it to her, and it remained her most beloved toy for a very long time.

Life was not all play though. Mishti also had to learn the rules of her new home. She was not allowed in the kitchen. If she went in the kitchen, Gilly shouted 'Out!' and looked a bit ferocious, and Mishti would reverse back into the doorway. There she would sit for hours. She loved eating and watching food being made. For her it was like watching the best movie ever. Then she also had to learn not to beg for food at the dining table. If she crept too close, Gilly would say 'Doooor!' very firmly, and Mishti soon learned that this meant she had to sit further away. Helping herself to food from the table was also banned, as she learned on her first ever Diwali.

That afternoon, Gilly and Mark were sitting with guests, a big, big plate of the finest kaju barfi on the table in front of them. The barfi was still on the table by the sofa when Gilly and Mark went to see off their guests. When they came back, it was missing. The plate was empty except for a few crumbs. Mishti meanwhile was looking strangely content, her eyes gleaming as if she had done something particularly clever. It wasn't hard to put two and two together. 'Bad dog!' said Gilly, pretending to be angry, 'Very, very bad dog!' Not only had she eaten from the table, sugar was really very bad for dogs. Mishti's ears drooped but her eyes were not saying sorry.

'Well, Mishti,' said Mark, who was highly amused, 'Your name means "sweet" and today you have lived up to your name. What a naughty girl you are!'

# MISHTI THE SHREDDER

Mishti had worked out for herself how to get people out of bed in the morning. You could be lying happily asleep and Mishti would hop up beside you, and lie with her full weight across your stomach. If that failed, she would climb on your chest and lick your face. Mishti had a very, very long, pink tongue useful for this purpose. So you had to get up. Once you were out of bed, Mishti leapt and barked until she was taken for a walk. Mishti loved her walks, but in Delhi to get to the best parks, you had to drive. And this was the problem. One thing Mishti had learned from her long Ambassador journeys was that she Hated Cars.

So she would be thrilled to see Gilly pick up her

lead, and she would get in the car. But once the engine started she would become very nervous. Perhaps she thought she would be taken away and lose her new home. Whatever it was, she insisted on sitting in the driving seat. Now while Mishti was not a big Labrador, driving with her sitting in your lap was very difficult. She wouldn't keep still. It was impossible to see out of the window properly over her head, and it was almost impossible to change gear.

The alternative was to forget the big parks and walk in one of the small parks in the colony. Here, Mishti loved to chase anything that ran. She chased cats. She was so busy sprinting after one that she ran full tilt into barbed wire causing an unscheduled visit to the vet. And she just loved chasing squirrels.

One day Gilly managed to get Mishti to calm down, and she and Mark drove in a civilized manner to Lodi Gardens, one of Delhi's most beautiful parks set out around stone tombs some 500 years old. One of these tombs is at the top of a flight of steps, surrounded by a walled garden, and looks like a fort with turrets in the corners, and empty windows in the turrets. This tomb-garden is a good place to play ball and there are also lots of striped palm squirrels, or gilhari. Now, I don't know if you have noticed, but gilharis are very good at climbing up things, they can climb up tree trunks, and even old walls. After playing ball for a while, Mishti started chasing them. She ran after one that sped over the grass, into a turret, out of a window and up the wall outside. Mishti was running right behind as fast as an arrow. Unfortunately, she didn't have the mountaineering skills of the squirrel. So when she ran into the turret and jumped out of the window, she dropped like a stone. There was a loud yelp as she hit the ground some twelve feet below. Gilly and Mark ran to the window and looked down. Mishti looked up. Their eyes met. Gilly rushed down. After a few minutes Mishti managed, with some difficulty, to get to her feet but was now only using three legs.

'How will I explain this to Edward and Sally?' thought Gilly as she drove to the vet again.

The vet manipulated Mishti's leg and came to the

conclusion that it wasn't broken and told Gilly to apply a warm compress. So for the next few days Gilly spent a lot of time with Mishti and a hot water bottle. Finally, Mishti became a four-legged dog again and everyone heaved a big sigh of relief.

After that Mark and Gilly thought it better to stay at ground level when they went to Lodi Gardens. Mishti found other pursuits. In Lodi Gardens there were lots of Royal Palms, tall palm trees with great big fronds of leaves. Every so often a leaf fell with a huge thump. The leaf stems had great thick papery wings. Mishti immediately recognized that they had potential. They were good to play tug of war with. Mark and Gilly were very happy to play tug of war with Mishti, and Mishti tugged with all her might, but this was only half the fun. She discovered that she could tear long strips off the papery palm stems. Mishti the shredder was born. She pulled and she shook the leaves, she dragged them and tore them and worried them until her tongue was down to her knees with panting. Profoundly happy she sat down with her paws crossed and surveyed her

achievements. Then Mark and Gilly would pick up the shredded leaves and dump them on the nearest compost heap.

They didn't realize that this was a game with Consequences.

They decided to go for a weekend to the Glass House on the Ganges, a hotel run by friends of theirs, on the the banks of the Ganga in the hills above Rishikesh. They took permission from their friends to take Mishti with them, and packed the car with useful Mishti stuff including her blanket and a pressure cooker to cook the dal, rice and sabzi that she had for dinner. By now Mishti had been persuaded not to sit in the driving seat, but she still wasn't keen on car travel, and spent most of the journey on the floor of the car. Looking out of the window was still not for her.

Once they arrived, she was excited to explore her new surroundings. She had been born by the sacred Ganga but she had never seen it. In Mirzapur, the river is wide and slow and lies at the bottom of a high and very steep bank. Above Rishikesh the river is narrow, fast-flowing, glacier green and icy cold.

Mishti now saw the Ganga properly for the first time. It scared her. She ran away from even a splash of water. But then she discovered a new game. Digging. The sandy bank of the river was silvery and moist. Mishti dug faster and faster with her front paws. The sand flew all over her face and head and her nose was silver with it. 'This is awesome,' her eyes seemed to say. She was so excited that suddenly she stopped digging and began running round and round the hole she had dug, happier and happier, until, to the utter horror of Mark and Gilly, and before they could stop her, she raced towards the icy waters of the Ganga. In her excitement she now knew no fear and took a flying leap into the deepest and iciest pool around.

Gilly and Mark were dumbstruck. The glassy green water closed over Mishti. She sank deeper and deeper until only a tiny gold patch was visible. Then that disappeared. There was no sign of her. They couldn't believe it—she had gone forever. What would they say to Edward and Sally?

Then suddenly there was a smudge of gold beneath

the water. Her little head broke the surface. She had never swum in her life but she was swimming now. She was swimming for her life. Her paws were paddling as fast as they could, but she couldn't reach the bank near Mark and Gilly. The water was too fast. Instead she was heading diagonally to the shore, but she was making progress. Mark and Gilly ran down the bank of the river, and were there to meet Mishti when she finally emerged, very clean indeed and very wet, and panting hard. The effort had bent her tail. It was some months before she could straighten it again.

Mark and Gilly were thrilled to have Mishti safe and sound and were about to give her a big hug, when she shook herself so vigorously that she sprayed them all over with Ganga water.

After her great leap, Gilly and Mark decided to keep her firmly on the lead when she was near the river.

In the evening, Gilly cooked Mishti's dinner on a small stove in the cottage room where they were staying. After Mishti had eaten, it was Mark and Gilly's turn to eat. But they didn't want to go the restaurant and leave Mishti in the room alone. There was no saying what she would get up to. So they took her with them. The problem was that in a new place, Mishti's sit-and-staying was not as good as it was at home. So she ended up very close to and sometimes under the table, and some of the other guests didn't seem to like this. The next night they decided to put her in the car, leaving the windows open for cool, fresh air. She seemed quite happy as she could see into the restaurant from the front seat.

They had a very pleasant dinner. Meanwhile Mishti found something to keep herself busy.

After dinner Mark and Gilly came to fetch her. When they opened the door of the car they noticed that the seat seemed to be covered with confetti. Tiny bits of paper were everywhere. Gilly examined them closely. They looked familiar.

Mishti had shredded their driving maps of Kumaon and Garhwal. Then they noticed the gearstick. The top of it was a well-chewed, tooth-marked, gooey mess.

Gilly said, 'Bad Mishti!' but really felt it was her fault for leaving Mishti in the car. Mishti herself looked bright-eyed at her evening's work, and very happy to be on holiday and to have been the only one of them to have taken a dip in the sacred river. Together the three of them walked up the dark path to their cottage, while the stars shone overhead, and all was silent but for the rushing of the River Ganga.

# MISHTI THE SOCIAL BUTTERFLY

Nunu, Mana and Tushi gave Mishti the name 'Social Butterfly', because she was one.

She was a social butterfly with dogs and with humans. Of course if you see a dog and want to pet it, you should always ask the owner so you do it in the right way. Without meaning to you can scare the dog, and it might snap at you. Gilly was glad that children asked before they patted Mishti. And Mishti was always glad to be patted and stroked.

She was very friendly with dogs too. Whenever she saw a new dog, she would stand as tall as she could, her ears would go forward, she would smile in a doggy way, her eyes shining and her tail going tick-tock back and forth as she trotted off to say hello and begin social smelling.

Her friends were uncountable.

Next door was Suki the black Labrador. Suki's humans were always coming to ask where she was because whenever their door was left open, Suki would sneak out and round the corner to see Mishti. She would scratch on the wire netting of the kitchen door until she was let in. Mishti and Suki, gold and black, would then play mad wrestling games round the sitting room. To prevent things getting broken, Gilly would let them out in the garden, and then, to protect the flower pots from being broken, she let them into the road outside, which was closed off and didn't have any traffic.

Not far away was was Simba the golden Labrador. He lived with Mark and Gilly's close friends, Shobita and Samiha. He was fed and walked by their cook Jugal, who came from a place not far from Mirzapur. Jugal would feed him fresh rotis straight from the

tavva, and as a result Simba ONLY liked fresh rotis from Jugal's hands. Jugal's wife Saraswati said rather sarcastically that she wished Jugal had taken as much care of his own children. But Jugal was unmoved. He taught Simba Bhojpuri and when it was time for the great festival of Chhat Puja, he would take him for the celebrations with the rest of the family.

Mishti and Simba would spend hours playing and licking each other's faces while their humans chatted. One lunchtime Simba managed to do something Mishti never could. Samiha had accidentally shut him in her bedroom. Instead of barking to be let out, he managed all on his own to push across the bolt at the bottom of the door and lock himself in. Having done that, however, he couldn't work out how to unbolt the door. Mishti stood outside and sniffed and barked until everybody took notice. As they found the door locked from the inside, they all trooped on to the balcony and peered in through the bedroom window. Inside Simba was sitting near the door staring intensely at the bolt as if trying to work out what to do with it. 'Push the bolt across!' they shouted. But Simba only wagged his tail. In the end, Jugal had to break the wire netting over the window and climb in to rescue him. That was a very memorable lunchtime.

Mishti was also a founding member of the Doggy Panchayat in Lodi Gardens. Most dogs in Delhi are street dogs. Lodi Gardens had lots of street dogs who lived there and were looked after by the people who walked there. Among Mishti's special garden-dog friends were Zorro, who had a white Z mark on his forehead, and Scruffy who was, well, scruffy. The garden-dogs were very much at ease with the people who came to the park with their dogs for morning walks. Among those dogs were Kookie the beagle, and a wolf-like hound called Pippa who had lived in Ethiopia, and the handsomest Labradors in the whole of Delhi, Kutus and Doogie, who were three times as big as Mishti. Their humans would get together near a fountain surrounded by trees every morning for a chat while their dogs played. Even early in the morning they would discuss the Future of India.

Favourite games included catch, chase the ball, and tag. Mishti would crouch like a lion, waggle her bottom, and Zorro would lower his head, walk up to Mishti and then race off in a big circle. Mishti would run after him as fast as her legs would take her. Sometimes she would catch him and roll him over, but more often she wouldn't and they would start the chase again. This was a good game, but in the summer there was a better one.

Then the fountain played and filled with a pool of cool water. The Panchayat dogs would jump in it and cool down. Gilly and Mark would throw a ball or a stick into the fountain and Mishti would jump in with a huge splash and jump out with the ball or stick and bring it back.

Mishti even taught a garden-dog how to play this game. Little Friend was a beautiful ginger spanielly sort of dog, very gentle and lonely. She seemed to have been abandoned. Some people don't realize that a dog needs a lot of looking after and caring for, and occasionally dogs that people didn't want anymore were just abandoned in Lodi Gardens. This was very cruel and Little Friend always seemed to be missing her human family. She was very shy, but Mishti made friends with her and led her to the Panchayat. Little Friend stood looking at the fountain from a distance, but Mishti kept going into the water and then coming back, until she plucked up courage to hesitantly step in herself. She sat down gently in the cool water. Little Friend no longer looked sad, and she began to join in the Panchayat's water games every day.

Labradors are specially bred for swimming. So Mark and Gilly thought that it was a shame that the only proper swimming Mishti had done was when she had nearly drowned in the River Ganga.

The River Jumna in Delhi was so black and stinking that no one and no dog should swim in it. So they had to think of somewhere outside Delhi.

They had some friends with a house near Dehradun. At the bottom of their garden was a stream, with rock pools, some of which were quite deep. The water there was still clean. So one weekend, Gilly and Mark packed up their car with Mishti things, including dog biscuits and the pressure cooker, and set off. By now Mishti had agreed to look out of the window for a bit, but still spent most of the journey on the car floor.

There were lots of dogs that already lived in the house in Dehradun, and also a cow called Lakshmi. Mishti found Lakshmi most interesting.

Early in the morning Mark, Gilly and Mishti climbed down to the river through orchards of fruit trees. Mishti tiptoed through the shallows and looked very pleased with herself. But after her Ganga experience, she wouldn't go near the deep pools where her paws couldn't touch the bottom. The weather was very hot. And so for her own sake and for Mishti's, Gilly stepped into the deepest pool. The clear, cold water came above her waist. She pushed her arms forward and began to swim. Swimming in natural places under the open sky is so much more enjoyable than a swimming pool, she thought. Mishti stood with her head cocked to one side, watching. 'Mishti! Come here!' called Gilly. Mishti thought about it for a few moments. Then she too slipped into the pool and doggy paddled towards Gilly. 'Good girl!' said Gilly. Mishti was careful to keep her head above the surface so no water went into her nose.

After a while Gilly got out, and Mishti followed her. Then dripping Gilly picked up a big stick and threw it as far as she could into the deep pool. Without thinking twice Mishti jumped after it, held it in her mouth, then doggy paddled round and swam back towards Gilly to give her the stick. 'Well done!' said Gilly giving Mishti a pat. They played this game until they were both tired. Then they climbed up the steep hill back to the house, and Gilly gave Mishti a good rub down with an old towel while Mishti tried to play towel tug-of-war.

Then they had lunch. It is very important that Labradors, who love food, don't have too much as they can easily get fat and unhealthy. So while Gilly and Mark had sabzi and roti, she stood obediently by the table waiting, and as soon as they had eaten they threw Mishti some slices of cucumber, which had few calories but were very healthy, and Mishti was happy to catch every slice they threw for her and munch it crunchily.

This was also the holiday when Mishti learned to be quiet. Gilly loved birdwatching, and it is very important when you are watching birds, or any wild animal, to be very still and quiet. Together they would climb down to the stream. Then Mishti would sit beside Gilly as she took out her binoculars and examined the rocks ahead, where the river was shallow and bubbly. Every day they would see a bird that liked swimming as much as Mishti did. It was called a dipper, and it was small and brown. It could walk underneath the water, darting around and pecking at the insects and worms that were its food. It kept its feathers well oiled so that they didn't get sodden, and between dips would flit between the river stones.

Gilly was very pleased that Mishti was beginning to calm down, and could be her birdwatching companion.

# MISHTI THE MUCKY PUP

Mishti began to go birdwatching with Gilly and her friends to Delhi's Okhla bird sanctuary on the Jumna river. In those days the sanctuary had not been surrounded by electricity pylons and buildings, and even though the water was black and smelly, there were thousands and thousands of ducks and geese, and purple moorhens and flamingoes, and falcons and harriers and all kinds of birds. The water was covered with them, and great flocks would wheel in the skies. There were wild mammals too. Black-naped hares would scoot across the path as you drew close, families of mongoose would play by the side of the road, and often a herd of nilgai, the biggest Indian antelope, would wander through the reed beds.

This was also where the farmers from the nearby village brought their buffaloes to graze and to wallow. You had to look left and right before you crossed any of the paths as you were very likely to meet these huge black animals, some of them very frisky.

Gilly was careful not to let Mishti go into the water or too near the buffaloes.

One day she, Mishti, her friend Jenny and Pippa, the dog from Ethiopia, were at the sanctuary. Gilly was counting the white and grey bar-headed geese that had arrived from their breeding grounds in Ladakh, and listening to their haunting honking. Suddenly Jenny nudged her. 'Look!' she said. Gilly turned to see where she was pointing. Instead of an interesting bird like a black-necked stork or a glossy ibis, she saw Mishti lapping up buffalo potty like it was the best mutton curry. She screamed, having worked out that this was the best way of grabbing Mishti's attention. Mishti at once realized she'd been seen doing something she shouldn't, and began eating even more quickly. Gilly raced towards her and Mishti abandoned her meal and sped down the path. She knew what was coming. 'Bad Mishti!' shouted Gilly, catching up with her and putting her on her lead.

So began Mishti's dirtiest habit.

The Okhla bird sanctuary was only one of the places that Gilly and Mark took Mishti. They always took her with them to watch the polo that was played on a large ground next to Delhi racecourse. Polo is a game played by ponies and people. The people on the ponies have long-handled mallets that they use to hit a ball. There are goals at each end of the polo ground and if your team hits the ball through the goal then they score. It's a very difficult game to play, and it is wonderful to watch the ponies galloping after the ball.

A lot of very smartly dressed people used to come to see the polo in Delhi. The women wore designer clothes and high-heeled shoes and lots of make-up, and even the men looked very fashionable. Mark and Gilly never looked very smart but they had one thing that made them acceptable. They had Mishti. It was traditional to bring your Labradors to see the polo.

Mishti loved it. Gilly would bring her water bowl in case she got thirsty, and she would sit beside them and watch closely, especially when the ponies came galloping past. She liked the smell of the polo ponies, and noted that ponies did potty as they were playing and the grass was dotted with piles of poo.

Being a very cute Labrador, Mishti attracted all the children in the stands, and as the parents of the children gave them biscuits and crisps to keep them quiet during the match, Mishti was able to sample these too. So the polo was one of her favourite outings.

One day she went to see a very important match. It was the final of the tournament. A maharani had come, dressed in a chiffon sari and pearls, to give away the silver trophy and medals to the winners. While the table with all the prizes was being laid out in front of the stands, some of the spectators walked out on to the field. Gilly and Mark noted a couple of very handsome Labrador puppies among them, and thought Mishti the social butterfly would like to meet them. The puppies' owners' were very proud of their puppies because they had cost over a lakh of rupees each. Mishti was a true egalitarian, and didn't care what price tag was put on a dog. For her they were just two more puppies to play with. So she began to play. Gilly and Mark began to discuss the best way to train a Labrador with the puppies' owners. So they didn't notice when Mishti suddenly left and went running over the polo ground towards the table with all the silver prizes on it. And they didn't notice when she reached it and stopped just beside it and just in front of the maharani in her chiffon sari and pearls. And most importantly, they didn't notice the expression of the Very Important People when they saw Mishti put down her head and start devouring a huge pile of pony poo just beside the table, as if she was trying to break the world record for poo eating. But the expensive puppies' owners did. They said, rather disgustedly, 'Oh, look what your dog is doing!'

Gilly turned, and saw Mishti with her nose buried in a mountain of poo. 'Excuse me,' she said, and ran towards the table, grabbing Mishti by the collar and

pulling her away and, at the same time, turning bright pink with embarrassment.

They didn't stay for the high tea after that match, even though Mishti liked pakoras and cucumber sandwiches.

The next time Gilly took Mishti to the vet, she told him about Mishti's dirtiest habit. The vet said that this was called a 'depraved appetite' and meant there must be something missing in Mishti's diet. He gave Gilly a pot of multi-vitamins and minerals to see if that would help. Gradually, Mishti stopped running after poo, and finally stopped eating it all together. Mark and Gilly were very relieved.

# MISHTI THE MILK BAR

Mishti's fans were always asking when she was going to have puppies. Finally the time came. Mishti was pregnant and bulging slightly at the sides. Obviously there was a queue of puppies waiting for the right time to pop out.

Gilly had borrowed a whelping frame from her friend Belinda, whose father had owned many generations of Kolkata Labradors including Mishti's great-great-grandfather. The frame sat on the floor and had a rail inside it high enough and deep enough so that if a mother dog sat down against the edge of the frame her puppies would not be squashed but be pushed underneath the rail. Gilly had read that Mishti would want to have her pups in a quiet dark place, and so she put the frame on the spare bedroom floor on top of some old newspapers and hung a sheet over it.

Everyone was watching Mishti very closely. Finally she started panting heavily. The vet said she was in labour. That morning passed and so did the afternoon, and then the evening. Mishti was still panting and there were still no puppies. Gilly tried to persuade Mishti to sit in the whelping frame, but Mishti didn't seem at all impressed by the makeshift tent. Finally at three a.m., she jumped on to the bed in the spare bedroom and her puppies were born, slipping out one by one, headfirst, wrapped up in slippery parcels, until there were four. And then one more came out the difficult way, feet first, but he too made it safely into the world.

Gilly gently cleaned out their mouths and made sure they could breathe. They were tiny and silky. Their eyes were tightly shut and the pads of their paws were as pink as their tongues. They made little mewing noises.

She naturally expected Mishti to know what to do.

After all, wasn't it instinct? Mother animals must know how to look after their babies.

However, Mishti had been taken from her mother when she was very young and had never had puppies before. To start with she was happy to lick them clean, but then when she saw them properly she growled and snapped at them as if they were her world's worst enemies. She didn't seem to know who or what they were. For the next few hours Gilly made sure the puppies were warm and fed them drops of starter puppy milk she had kept for emergencies. Mishti wanted nothing to do with her pups.

When it was light Gilly rang the vet who told her how important it was that the puppies should drink Mishti's first milk. The first milk that mother animals feed their babies is very rich and full of strength to fight against disease. The vet said he had an idea. He was soon there with his black box of medicines. He looked at the puppies and said they were fine. And then he looked at Mishti and handed a red muzzle to Gilly. 'You will have to use this,' he said.

Mishti had never worn a muzzle before as it was to stop dogs biting and she had never looked like she was going to bite anyone. Now there seemed no choice. Gilly pulled the muzzle over Mishti's nose and fastened the straps behind her ears. Then she laid Mishti on her side and quickly lined up all five puppies, nose first, against her teats. The puppies were hungry, and although they couldn't see because puppy eyes don't open until they are two weeks old, they found their way to her teats and hungrily sucked her milk.

Mishti had the good sense to lie still, but the moment the puppies were back in the whelping frame and the muzzle was off she growled and snarled again. Throughout the day, Gilly kept putting on the muzzle, and then lining up the puppies against Mishti so they could drink milk. By nighttime she was exhausted. She took off Mishti's muzzle one last time and told her, 'Mishti, these are your puppies. I can't stay awake any longer. Now it's up to you. Please don't eat them. Goodnight.'

Saying this she went to bed and fell asleep immediately. When she woke the next morning she was worried. What would she find? Would the puppies still be alive?

Quietly she crept to the door of the spare bedroom and peeped in.

Mishti was lying very comfortably in the whelping frame. Where were the puppies? Two were almost hidden, lying under the protective ledge of the frame, two more were lying next to her and one was having his tummy licked. Their little stomachs moved softly with their breath. They were all there! They were all alive! All was well!

Left on her own that night, Mishti had made the decision to become the perfect milk bar. The next few weeks were very enjoyable. Mishti was very happy because she was extra hungry and was given extra big meals. She was very careful how she sat down and didn't squash a single puppy, and seemed to go into a trance when she was feeding them. They seemed to be hungry or sleepy, mainly hungry. The puppies were all golden and soon the pads of their paws turned from pink to black. When their eyes opened they were pure blue. There were two girls and three boys. The world was their mother and she was also their first climbing frame.

Members of the Mishti fan club were eager to see and hold the puppies. The first to arrive were Nunu, Mana and Tushi. Mishti did whirlytails to welcome them. When she was ordinarily happy she wagged her tail from side to side, but when she was especially happy, Mishti drew circles in the air. She was happy for them and, in fact, for anyone to hold the puppies. The children, their parents and grandparents, and Gilly and Mark's friends, all came to see Mishti and her pups.

Mishti licked the five puppies and kept them so clean that you wouldn't know there was a puppy in the house. They began to walk on less wobbly feet. They kept growing. Soon they were nearly big enough to climb out of the frame. Then they did. They began to explore the world around them. It was getting easier to tell them apart, and so they got their first names. Brains got his name because he was so clever at getting to drink Mishti's milk first. Sultan was named after his grandfather in Mirzapur. He was the first to be born, and the biggest and sucked as hard as a vacuum cleaner. Snowy was the liveliest and the naughtiest and was white-gold and very Mishti-like. Soni was more deep gold and the quietest of them all. And then there was Kim, the last born, who came out of his mother backwards, and was the smallest and weakest of all. He was biscuit-brown and very mischievous.

# A HOUSE FULL OF PUPPIES

The spare room now became their playroom. Gilly rolled up the rugs and stood the beds on their side, and bought a few small squeaky toys from the pet shop for them to play with. For the fan club, Gilly put out a couple of muras to sit on. The puppies ran after the toys—as did Mishti (she thought they had been bought for her)—but Mishti was still their favourite toy of all. She didn't mind even when three of them climbed on her head at the same time.

Now they had to learn to eat solid food. The vet said the puppies would be happy with moong ki dal ki khichri. So every day Gilly made a pot of khichri (without salt), and added some chopped hard-boiled egg, some paneer, and the calcium and vitamins the vet had recommended. Then every few hours she would spoon some of the mixture on five saucers, and carry them out on a tray to the verandah just outside the spare room. As soon as the puppies saw Gilly with the tray they ran after her. Gilly held the tray and said, 'Sit!' All five puppies would sit down, and all five puppies would look up with big hungry eyes. Gilly was very impressed that they had already learned to sit. However, they had not learned to stay.

As soon as she put the tray down the puppies rushed to the dishes. There was one saucer of food for each puppy, but they all seemed to think that the food in the next dish was better than theirs. So there was a mad rush between plates. Gilly had to keep picking the puppies up and putting them in front of the right dishes so that she knew that all of them, especially Kim, who had some catching up to do, had enough food.

The verandah outside the spare room was very small but very useful. Gilly kept the puppies there when she was cleaning the room. As they grew bigger there was a lot of cleaning to do. Although Gilly knew that until a puppy is six months old, it can't totally control its urge to susu, she thought she would try and teach them. So after every meal and long sleep, she took them out into the little patch of garden to relieve themselves and praised them when they did, saying, 'GOOD dog!' Inside the room she spread out newspaper so the puppies would susu on it. At least that was what they were meant to do according to a book Gilly had read.

However, the puppies hadn't read that book. They just tore up the newspaper, chewed it to a pulp and ate it.

Even though they were now on solid food they still liked Mishti's milk. But as they were now much bigger, Mishti began to feel that she needed some time away from her demanding pups. To help her, Gilly decided to make a barrier in the doorway of the spare room that Mishti could jump over when she needed to, but the pups couldn't. She found some old cardboard boxes and wedged them into the doorway. The puppies tried to get out. They couldn't. But Mishti hopped over easily.

That night Mishti came to sleep on the floor in Gilly's bedroom. Gilly was happy to have Mishti back again as she loved to hear her contented breathing, and occasional barks in her sleep as she dreamed. But around three a.m. Gilly's eyes opened. She didn't realize what had woken her. She looked over the side of the bed. It was dark. In that darkness she could just make out five small pairs of eyes, all open wide, looking back at her. She leapt up, having a vision of five puppies susuing in her bedroom, and ran out of the room. The puppies, thinking this was a wonderful chasing game, ran after her.

Gilly saw that left with time on their hands, they had managed to move the boxes just enough to make a puppy path to freedom. Gilly said, 'Goodnight, puppies!' shut them back inside the spare room, closing the door firmly, and went back to bed.

There were still two weeks to go.

Some breeders give puppies away to new owners when they are four weeks old. However, it is much better for the puppies if they stay longer with their mothers. Gilly and Mark thought they would keep the puppies until they were six weeks old, but Belinda—whose family had bred Mishti's great-great-grandfather—said eight weeks would be better. By carefully planning their susu breaks, Gilly had managed to enlarge their world to outings in the sitting room. She and Mark, and Bubbly who cooked for them and Kaka who drove the car and helped out, and Tushi and Nunu and Mana and all the fan club loved to watch them.

Six Labradors playing in a sitting room is a wonderful sight. Waves of puppies played across the room. Mishti now found that they made wonderful toys themselves. They would chase her and she would chase them and roll them over and play mad wrestling with them, with lots of pretend growling and barks. The puppies found Mishti's old water bowl and made a toy of it, picking it up and running round the room, and chewing it. They now had their milk teeth. Dogs, like humans, have one set of teeth when they are young and grow bigger stronger ones as they get older.

Gilly and Mark meanwhile were looking for good homes—people who would look after the puppies well. If you decide to look after any living thing, you should do it well. A dog needs to be looked after from its early years to its old age. It's a big responsibility. Gradually they found good people, and one by one their owners came to collect them.

First went Sultan, then Brains (who later travelled with the army to Ladakh), and then there was Snowy, who went by train to stay in Mirzapur with Edward and Sally. Belinda and her mother Anne decided they had space in their home for one more dog, and Kim, who had grown wonderfully and was as big as any of his brothers, went to stay with them. He was so big he filled Anne's arms when she came to take him home.

The house now seemed very empty. But Mishti would never be on her own again. Gilly and Mark decided to keep Soni, the quietest of the pups. She occasionally limped and they thought she would need a lot of love and looking after. So Mishti bade farewell to four of her pups but did not seem sad, because she had Soni.

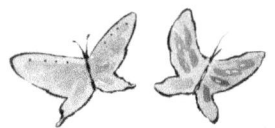

# MISHTI AND THE BATHTUB

Up until now Soni had been with her brothers and sisters. Now she had just her mum, and her mum slept in Gilly's bedroom, so Soni did too. The first night Soni explored a bit, and jumped on the bed. She decided the only place she was comfortable was on Gilly's pillow, and Gilly found she had four puppy paws waving in her face as Soni rolled on to her back. She put Soni on her bed on the floor, but whenever Gilly woke up Soni was next to her. Gradually, she moved her down the bed until both Mishti, who loved nothing better than the feeling of a clean cotton bedspread beneath her, and Soni were under her feet rather than in her face.

As Soni grew up she had all the jabs from the vets that would save her from the dangerous diseases that are around—diseases like rabies and distemper. This meant visits to the vet and it soon became clear that Soni's attitude to the vet was very different from Mishti's.

Mishti's experiences as a puppy had left her with a fear of vets as well as cars, and this fear had turned her into an ace escape artiste. Once she realized she was walking to the vet's she would immediately go into reverse gear, slip her head out of her collar and race off. To stop this Gilly bought her a smart red harness to wear instead of a collar. The harness held her round her shoulders and the top of her legs and seemed very secure. She looked very cute in it and enjoyed going for walks. But the moment she found out she was going to her least favourite place, she would wriggle and wriggle and in ten seconds you were holding an empty harness and she was gone. So Mishti was made to wear both a collar and a harness when she went to the vet's. Gilly and Kaka both went to hold her and took a handful of dog biscuits as bribes. Still she fought and protested all she could.

Soni in contrast had known the vet ever since the day she was born. Occasionally he would come to the house when they were puppies. There was the day when Gilly found them scratching because somehow they had got lice. These looked very like the lice that Mana, Nunu and Tushi brought back from school in their hair and took a lot of getting rid of with nit combs and medicated shampoo. Perhaps the puppies had caught lice from the girls? However, the vet said that dog lice were different from human ones, and popped round with a kind of spray, suitable for puppies, that dealt with the problem. So to Soni vet meant Friend with a capital F.

The vet's clinic was in a small market and a queue of dogs waited to see him. None of them looked very happy to be there. Soni in contrast strained at the lead. While Kaka kept a tight hold on Mishti, Soni just wouldn't keep quiet. She longed to see her Friend and to be patted and petted and given a biscuit. 'Hi, I'm here!' she barked enthusiastically, 'Let me in!' she barked joyfully, and then when her time came she squealed with pleasure before she was lifted on to the table to have her jab or her bottom cleaned. Her noisiness was embarrassing. No other dog in the whole of Delhi was so pleased to see the vet.

Watching Soni, Mishti became less scared. And Soni helped Mishti in other ways too. One of the best parks in Delhi is called Nehru Park. It has huge open spaces and woods full of flowering trees and the best butterfly-made-of-pansies in the whole city. It also has lots of interesting rocks to climb over. In between two sets of rocks was a bridge made of wire and wood that swayed and creaked a lot as you walked over it. Mishti would come to the edge of it and stop, rooted to the spot. Not all the dog biscuits in the Windsor Pet Shop could get her on to that bridge.

For Soni the very same bridge held no fear at all. It was just another adventure. She wandered across, sniffing all the way. Both Mishti and Soni loved to sniff, for them it was like reading the newspapers. Dogs can smell all sorts of things that we can't. Seeing Soni sniffing, Mishti followed her on to the bridge and was never afraid of it again.

So sometimes Soni taught her mother something. But sometimes it was the other way round.

Once a year comes the prettiest of Indian festivals—Diwali. In the old days people would light diyas made of clay, and how beautiful they looked in the dark, moonless night. And they would line their roofs with candles, and have a few fireworks. But as Delhi grew, the sound of firecrackers and 'bombs' became deafening. They terrified birds and animals and babies and made life unpleasant for old people and people who had difficulty breathing because of all the smoke, and lots of other people as well. As much as a festival of lights, it had become a festival of noise and smoke.

Mishti was petrified every Diwali, and so instead of celebrating with friends, Bubbly and Kaka would organize a small puja at home for Mark and Gilly, and they would all put out some clay diyas, and then Gilly would settle down to comfort Mishti until it was all over. Unfortunately, Mishti's fear was infectious. Soni found it as scary as Mishti and they would both tremble with terror, and look for places to hide the furthest away from the noise. The fan club would sometimes come to give them a cuddle. They would close the curtains, and turn on the TV so the noise outside was muffled as much as possible.

One Diwali, Mana came to stay. She was growing into a very slim, tall girl, with long hair that fell in soft curls. She immediately put her bag in the spare room. The spare room had an attached bathroom and in that bathroom, wedged against the wall, was an antique bath. It was made of cast iron with four short legs to keep its round belly off the ground and it was very heavy. Some years ago Gilly had found it standing unwanted on the side of the road and brought it home. It was, no doubt, a very good bathtub but it was so heavy that it took four strong men to get it into the bathroom. Mana's sister, Tushi, had then spent many happy hours in it wearing her swimming costume and cap and pretending to swim.

That Diwali, Mana casually left the bedroom door open when Gilly called her to share some delicious milk cake and barfi. At that moment there was a humungous 'BANG!', then another, and another. It was as if war had broken out. The dogs shivered, crouched low to the ground and then ran out of the sitting room. Gilly and Mana wiped their fingers and went to look for them. They found Soni under Mana's bed. But they couldn't find Mishti anywhere.

They looked all over the house. She wasn't in any room. Where could she be?

Then Mana, who always had a lot of imagination, looked in her bathroom again.

'Gilly! I've found her!'

Mana was staring at the bathub.

She pointed and said, 'Look underneath.'

They both knelt down and peered under the belly of the bath. Crammed into the far corner next to the wall was a petrified Mishti, her tongue fully extended, panting with terror.

'How on earth did she get in there?' asked Gilly.

'And how can we ever get her out?' replied Mana, her big eyes wide as could be.

'BANG! CRASH!'

The boys at the back of the house were exploding bombs again. Gilly and Mana had asked them not to do it so close, but they hadn't listened.

There was no question of extracting Mishti, so they tried to calm her down as best they could. Mana spread a durrie on the bathroom floor and lay down on it, so their eyes were on the same level. She said some soothing things, and then when that made no difference, fetched her mobile. She had a long playlist of her favourite music. And she decided to play it to Mishti to distract her. While Mana lay on the durrie, Gilly went and brought dog treats. She climbed into the bath and, holding a treat, managed to push her arm between the corner of the bath and the wall and offer it to Mishti. Mishti was too scared to eat but at least Gilly could pat her nose.

The hours passed. Nine o'clock. Ten o'clock. Around eleven, Mishti was persuaded to eat three dog treats. Her tongue wasn't so far out, and her panting wasn't so bad. But she refused to budge. At midnight

Gilly and Mana decided to have a nap. Soni came out from under the bed and cuddled up to them. There were still explosions but they weren't nearly so noisy. At two a.m., there was a metallic 'Boing!' as Mishti tried to get out from under the bath and discovered she couldn't. Gilly, Mana and Soni, jumped up and went to the bathroom.

Mishti had no hope of getting out. She was not only wedged under the bath, she was trapped between its legs and the wall. Gilly clasped her forehead, stood back and tried to think of four strong men she could phone at two a.m. on a holiday to shift a bathtub.

But Mana was Mana. She had known Mishti since she was a little girl and Mishti was a puppy. Mishti was her Friend. Suddenly with superhuman strength she grabbed the rim of the bath at the opposite end to the taps, where Mishti was trapped. Her muscles strained. She gritted her teeth. The bathtub clanged as she lifted it an inch and dragged it a couple of inches to one side. Mishti was just waiting for such a moment. Super fast, she wriggled backwards, the way she had come.

Gilly helped drag her out.

And then there she was free. FREE!

All four of them were so happy. Gilly and Mana had another piece of barfi, and they cuddled the dogs, while Mana snapchatted the evening's events to her very large circle of friends. Then at last all four of them went to sleep.

And that was the last time the bathroom door was left open on Diwali.

# TWO DOGS FOR A WALK

If you are used to taking one dog for a walk, taking two can be something of a shock, especially if the second dog thinks you like being dragged along at a hundred kilometres an hour at the end of the lead. The second dog in this case was Soni. As we have seen, when she was a young puppy, she was quiet. She was also small. But she grew and she grew until she was much bigger than her mother but just as bouncy. Lots of people they met in the park thought that Mishti was the puppy and Soni was her mother.

Mishti, however, was well trained. She had learned in Mirzapur how to walk to heel and in Delhi she had learned sit and stay, and catch and shake hands and not to go into the kitchen or beg at the table. Heeling meant that when she was on the lead, and told 'Heel!' she would walk beside the human at the other end of her lead and not drag him or her along at a hundred kilometres an hour. Soni had to learn this.

Now undoubtedly the best way to teach a dog is to get hold of their humans and teach them how to talk to their dogs. In many countries, 'puppy schools' mean 'human-with-puppy schools'. The teachers teach the humans so well that before a puppy is six months old he is heeling and lying down and rolling over on command. There were no puppy schools where Mark and Gilly lived, but among the thousands of books in their house was one about training dogs. So Mark and Gilly read the book and set about training Soni.

Not far from their house was Humayun's Tomb, a huge building of white, red and black stone, where lots of Mughals are buried, including Humayun the second Mughal Emperor. It stands in a garden, surrounded by a wall. Outside the eastern wall was a quiet park. It was long and had a small hill at one end which made it more interesting to run up and down. There were some trees, and no one to bother you. Here Gilly and Mark began the Soni training programme.

Since mother and daughter were so bouncy, the training sessions started with play. They played ball-ball, when Mark and Gilly would throw a tennis ball as far as they could and Soni and Mishti would race to be the first to reach it, and then race back with it. Then there would be stick-stick, when Mark and Gilly would throw a stick. This ended with stick tug-of-war, with Soni at one end of the stick and Mishti at the other, tugging and tugging with all their might until the stick broke.

After this Mark would take Mishti to one part of the park, and walk slowly round in a big circle, saying 'heel'. Mishti would fix her bright eyes on Mark and the pocket where she knew he had hidden a chapatti, and walk round and round by his side.

Gilly would put Soni on her lead, take her to another part of the park and make Soni sit on her left. Then she put her left foot forward, looked Soni

in the eye, gave her lead a little tug, and said, 'Soni, heel!' Soni set off beside Gilly but would soon start pulling ahead. Gilly then said, 'Back!' and gave a tug on the lead again. Soni rethought, and fell in step with Gilly, and then started pulling again. Gilly kept on trying. Then when Soni had finally managed to heel properly for a minute or so, Gilly would stop and say, 'Baith!' holding the lead tightly so that Soni would sit down beside her. When Soni got things right, Gilly praised her. Soni required a lot of tugging, and Gilly's shoulders got very tired, but slowly Soni began to get the idea.

After a few days, the time had come for the great test. Mark and Mishti stood by, watching to see if she would pass. Gilly walked Soni round twice with her lead on, then told her to sit. Soni sat, her eyes on Gilly and the small dog treat she had taken from her pocket. Gilly took off Soni's lead. This was the big moment. She put her left foot forward. 'Heel!' she said. Soni set off beside Gilly. Gilly kept on talking to her to keep her attention. 'Heel and back, heel and back, good girl!

Heel and back, heel and back!' Soni was walking right beside her even without her lead on. Gilly began to jog, and Soni jogged along beside her. Gilly jogged in a figure of eight and Soni stuck with her like a shadow. Gilly stopped. Soni stopped. And without Gilly saying a word she sat down close beside her.

'Well done, Soni!' said Gilly. 'Well done, Soni!' said Mark. 'Woof, woof!' barked Mishti, making little hops into the air to make her bark louder.

Now Mark wanted to try. He sat both Mishti and Soni down side by side on his left. 'Heel, Mishti! Heel, Soni!' he said. All three of them set off in one line together. Perfect discipline. How good they looked!

Just then a shrill chatter broke the air. Even though there was no wind the branches of the trees were swaying. All four of them stopped in their tracks. 'Oh, no!' thought Mark and Gilly.

'Oh, yes!' thought Mishti and Soni.

They forgot their training. Their discipline went out the window. Their hackles rose, their ears went forward and they were off like arrows towards the trees, barking and barking.

It was the Bandar Brigade, known to the residents' association as The Monkey Menace! Mark and Gilly now saw three or four red rhesus macaque monkeys sitting on the ground. One had a baby clinging on to her chest. Another was a big male. They looked at Soni and Mishti running towards them.

At the last minute before contact was made, the monkeys put out their long arms and climbed up into the trees, where they stayed just high enough to be out of reach and just low enough to make Mishti and Soni think they could jump up and catch them.

It had never occurred to Mishti and Soni to think what they would do if they did actually catch them.

Monkeys have big teeth. The male lowered his head and bared his at Mishti and Soni.

Gilly and Mark were afraid they would get bitten, and tried calling them back by shouting two of the dogs' favourite words, 'Biscuit! Roti!'

They both had sympathy for the Bandars. Before the city had grown so huge there had been plenty of space for humans and monkeys. Now the humans had

taken all their space, and they were living on the edge of human housing colonies. Only a week or so ago, a monkey had walked in through the kitchen door, opened the fridge, helped himself to the bananas in the fruit bowl, and then walked out again.

Mishti and Soni had been asleep in the bedroom, and knew nothing about it until Bubbly started screaming.

When the dogs didn't desert the Bandar Brigade for biscuits and roti, Gilly and Mark headed towards them, put on their leads and pulled them away so they wouldn't bother the Bandars any more. After a while they saw the Bandars wander off in the direction of the market. Then they heard the shouts of the sabzi-wallas and phal-wallahs as the Bandars helped themselves to fruit and veg.

Gilly and Mark wondered whether they should try to do more heeling with Mishti and Soni, but felt that enough was as good as a feast. Both they and the dogs were ready for breakfast. So they walked back from the park. But today Soni did not pull on her lead, and they all walked together as a team.

# MISHTI PLAYS WITH FIRE

Mishti loved digging. Sitting in muddy puddles satisfied her, and digging in mud delighted her. And so she, and sometimes Soni too, were often more black than golden. But they were never allowed into the house as black Labradors and always had to have a bucket bath first, and be rubbed with a towel while they played towel tug -of -war.

During the winter it's cold in Delhi, and so they were kept away from mud and baths as much as possible as they could easily catch a chill. But one winter day, they had a muddy morning and so Gilly had to wash them. She rinsed the shampoo out of their fur and rubbed them as dry as she could.

In the New Delhi dog parlours Gilly had seen people use hair dryers to dry dogs after a bath. But Gilly knew that Soni and Mishti didn't like them. In fact, they behaved as if hair dryers were evil aliens from outer space. When she pointed her hair dryer at them, they would bare their teeth and bark dementedly. Strangely enough, they had the same reaction to toothbrushes. If you held out a toothbrush and walked towards them they would bark hysterically and reverse out of the room. They didn't like the vacuum cleaner either.

So as Gilly wanted Soni and Mishti to dry off quickly after their bath, and a hair dryer was out of the question, she turned on the fan heater in the bedroom, shut the door to keep the warmth inside and went about her work. She thought they would settle down in their dog-beds in front of the heater and soon get dry.

It was a busy sort of day. Gilly started working on her laptop in their office room. Two carpenters were in the house making some more bookshelves, as the one thing Mark and Gilly had a lot of was books. Every day more arrived in the post. Piles of them lay around the house. It was a busy day upstairs too. There was an advertising office there and they had lots of visitors of their own.

About ten minutes after Gilly started work, Bubbly came in, panic-stricken.

'Bedroom ke darvaze ke niche se dhuan nikal rahi hai!' she cried.

Gilly ran across the sitting room to the bedroom. Smoke was indeed drifting out from underneath the door. Inside the dogs were barking. She threw the door open.

A terrifying sight met her eyes! The room was ablaze, flames leaping up the curtains. It was full of smoke. Her first priority was the dogs. She called, 'Mishti, Soni, come!' They trotted out immediately and once she saw they were safe, she shut them in the spare bedroom a good way away from the fire. Meanwhile Kaka had heard the noise. He immediately rushed to the Master Switch to turn off the electricity supply to the house. Gilly and Bubbly hurried to fill buckets with water. The carpenters came to help and, seeing the smoke, the office staff from upstairs ran downstairs with buckets. In just a few minutes there was a swift supply of buckets and pots of water pouring on to the flames. Soon the fire was extinguished.

At this point, Mark, who had been reading a very interesting and absorbing book in the garden, and so hadn't heard a thing, walked in, and asked, 'Has anything happened?'

Gilly and Bubbly looked at each other in amazement. Black smoke still swirled around the sitting room. The bedroom curtains and blinds and some books and papers, were destroyed and the ceiling and walls were black.

Everyone now had time to think. How could this have happened?

Gilly went to let the dogs out of the spare bedroom. She looked at both of them. Soni was very happy to be let out and ran around licking everyone within reach, a big smile on her face and her big, floppy ears set

forward. Mishti's eyes were sparkling with mischief. Mother and daughter were the only witnesses to the incident, and they weren't talking.

So Gilly went back to the scene of the crime and tried to piece the evidence together like a detective. There were plenty of clues. On the floor the fan heater looked like a painting by the artist Salvador Dali. It's plastic casing had melted into a bizarre, omelette-like shape. Around it were the noxious black remains of a dog-bed.

A light bulb turned on in Gilly's brain. She suddenly realized what must have happened.

Mishti was a playful dog. She played wrestling with her friends in the park, she played wrestling with her puppies, and she played wrestling with her round, cozy, foam dog-bed from the local pet-shop. Unlike the others, it couldn't wrestle back, so she could easily throw it around the room. After her morning walk she would on a normal day have a nap. However, the excitement of a muddy morning and a winter bath must have given her extra bounce. Gilly visualized

Mishti, a slightly manic look in her eyes, playing with the dog-bed until she tossed it on top of the fan heater. In only a minute or so the dog-bed must have caught fire, and after that the curtains.

There were lessons to be learned here. No more fan heaters anywhere near Mishti, and no more flammable dog-beds from the pet shop.

They had been so lucky that there were so many helpful people around. So lucky.

For the next week or so Gilly and Mark and the dogs slept in the spare bedroom. The painters moved into their bedroom, with all their paraphernalia. They kept on complaining about the number of coats of paint they needed to cover up the blackened ceiling and walls.

Mishti was a unique dog, thought Gilly. Some dogs saved their owners from danger, but Mishti had nearly burned the house down.

# MISHTI, SONI AND THE NEW CAR

It is quite true that it is twice as much fun having two dogs as having one. When you come home, there is twice as much excitement, there are twice as many licks, twice as many tail-wags, twice as many happy barks, and twice as many jumps for joy. Dogs are always there to welcome you home.

Of course, there are twice as many dog meals to be prepared, twice as many ears to be cleaned, twice as many feet to be checked for ticks, twice as much fur to be brushed, twice as much dog hair on the sofa (it's not called 'fur'-niture for nothing!), twice as many dog bowls to be washed, twice as many susu and potty walks, and twice as many visits to the vets. But these pale into insignificance before twice as much companionship and love.

And then there is the entertainment. Mishti was never one to sit quietly, and she regarded her daughter as a toy. She rolled her over and played mad wrestling with her all over the flat. But Soni, with her long face and huge floppy ears, was a lot bigger than Mishti. Soni soon began to think that Mishti was her toy, and would roll her on to her back, and win their wrestling bouts, until Mishti pretended to be angry and barked and snapped at her. Then Soni would settle down. She spent hours licking her mother's face and forehead, and Mishti would lick her back.

By now the house had a collection of squeaky toys, and rope toys, and old tennis balls, and, of course a football. And then came the new car.

Air pollution in Delhi was a big problem, and so when a friend offered Mark and Gilly the chance to try an electric car they thought it was a good idea. The car was as cute as a Labrador. It was very small and not at all heavy and was called a Reva. As it was so light it used very little energy to run and it took about as much space to park as a motorcycle. There was a back seat, but only Mana could use it and that too by lying on her back squeezed up like a ball. It was ideal for Mishti and Soni, and it became the best way to drive them around. The little car glided quietly, and instead of going fast, Mark and Gilly drove slowly to make the battery last as long as possible. Everywhere they went people asked them about the car. Some people thought it was a toy car, others wanted to know where the petrol went. They didn't know that you just plugged it in to charge it.

Driving it was truly as simple as if it was a child's toy. There were two pedals: one for stop (the brake) and one for go (the accelerator). On the dashboard was a round dial. If you turned the dial to F and pressed the accelerator, the Reva went Forward and if you turned it to R it went backwards (reversed). If you turned it to N, it was in neutral and wouldn't go anywhere.

One day, Gilly called the dogs to get into the car

to go for their walk. They leapt in. Soni jumped into the back seat, and Mishti decided for once to stay on the floor at the front. Then Gilly remembered she had left their leads indoors, and went to get them. Seeing the driver's seat unoccupied Soni immediately jumped into it. It was the best place to see what was going on and she always sat there while she was waiting for Mark and Gilly. Mishti, on the other hand, began to explore the floor of the car, and inched her way forward.

When Gilly came out of the house, the car was missing. She was totally bewildered. She looked left and right, and spotted the little white Reva trundling along towards the main road with Soni clearly visible in the driving seat. Her eyes opened wide. Without a moment's thought, she ran after the Reva as fast as her legs would carry her. She was no sprinter, but sheer panic gave her arrow-like speed. She drew level with the Reva, grabbed the door handle, swung open the door, pushed Soni from the driving seat, sat down, shoved Mishti from her position on top of the accelerator, and slammed on the brake.

Breathing heavily, her hands shaking, she looked at the dial. Instead of leaving it pointing to N for neutral, she had left it on F for Forward. It was her fault. She couldn't blame Mishti and Soni for driving without a license.

Luckily they hadn't hit anything.

She never left the Reva in Forward mode again. Soni and Mishti meanwhile seemed blissfully unaware that they had done anything particularly different. Even though there was hardly any space inside the Reva, they jumped all over Gilly and licked her, and still wanted their walk.

# MISHTI, SONI
# AND ARCHAEOLOGY

Gilly and Mark, Mishti and Soni loved walking in the park with the hill at the end where Soni had learned to heel. There were other parks nearby too, that were very jungly. Here they found peacocks, mynahs, green parakeets and green pigeons, magpie robins, francolins, hornbills, woodpeckers, ashy prinias, sunbirds, tiger butterflies, and dung-beetles with gleaming green shells. Sometimes they would sit quietly and watch a tiny dung -beetle roll a ball of dry poo nearly as big as itself to its hole.

One day, Soni and Mishti and Gilly were watching a dung-beetle when they heard a great bird-kerfuffle.

The mynahs and parakeets were kicking up an amazing racket, screeching and screeching, and the mynahs were gathering on the ground, all looking in one direction. The three of them went forward to investigate. Whatever it was, was near the mynahs. Gilly, being taller, saw it first. She held on tightly to the dogs' collars. On the ground in the sun lay a snake. It was at least five feet long and brown-black. It was a very splendid sight. They stood and watched until the snake finally got fed up with the birds and moved as swift as the wind across the ground and into the bushes.

He or she was a rat-snake. These are very useful because they eat rats, which generally are a nuisance to human beings. After that Gilly and the dogs walked very quietly in snaky places and saw the rat-snake sunbathing quite a few times.

It was fun to explore these jungly parks because people hardly ever went there. The branches of the kikar trees laced the sky and amar bel vines dangled like long spaghetti from their branches to the ground. But suddenly things began to change. Delhi was growing so fast it was becoming one of the biggest cities in the world, and no jungly place was left safe from humans wanting to build things. The government decided it wanted to build a road through the places that Mishti and Soni loved. It could easily have happened too, but local people who knew about history, discovered that there were important ruins in the jungle, too important to destroy. To save them, the road was stopped. But the jungle had been there so long that nobody, not even the people who stopped the road, knew exactly what was hidden among the trees and the bushes and the dung-beetle holes. Until that is, they began to dig.

The park where Soni learned to heel was the first target of the diggers. Labourers came and removed the grass, and dug a deep trench at the side of the hill. Mishti and Soni were keen to see what was at the bottom. They clambered down and Mishti did some extra digging of her own. What was it? A cave? Then they saw that under the hill was a row of high stone arches.

A long time ago the River Jumna had flowed where the park now was and what they thought was a hill had been a raised platform jutting into the riverbed. This would have been a way into the Humayun's Tomb gardens for people arriving by boat. The old doorway in the garden wall was still visible but had been blocked with stone. Over the years, grass had grown over the platform but on one side still stood an old tomb decorated with coloured tiles. Gilly and Soni and Mishti and Mark watched craftsmen repair the broken arches and Gilly imagined how nice it would have been to have sailed down the river in a boat with Soni and Mishti and moored below the tomb at the island. The dogs could have played splashing fetch games in the water. How lovely the sunrise would have been over the clean river, and how broad it would have been in the monsoon!

Once the arches had been found, the diggers began to look under the hummocks and slopes of the jungly places where the spaghetti vines hung from the kikar trees and clouds of red munias fed on tall grasses.

Early every morning Mark and Gilly and Mishti and Soni would go and see what they had found. One of the first things was an ancient well shaped like a wheel with spokes. When the earth was dug out from inside it, the well automatically filled up with water again. One day, the dogs followed a smell to a trench at the bottom of a ruined wall that had just been found under the earth. Mishti jumped down. She scrabbled and scraped in the mud. There was something smooth and long. Gilly climbed down after her, knelt down and brushed the earth from a long smooth stone. She looked at it carefully. This could only be a step. Below she could make out another one. So this must have been a flight of steps leading to a doorway in the wall of a lost garden. This was not the only lost garden discovered in this bit of jungle. The whole area would have been covered by them, the plants kept green by water from wells, and all of them standing by the beautiful, clean River Jumna that had changed its course on its own, but had become black and smelly thanks to human beings.

So much of Delhi was full of history, but only in a very few places had people stopped to look and see what they could find hidden in the soil. Mishti and Soni and Gilly and Mark were especially lucky to be there when things lost for hundreds of years were being uncovered and every day was a fresh adventure.

They had special fun at the nursery, next door to the lost garden with the steps. The far end of the nursery had been so jungly that they had never been able to explore it before. Now buildings and archways were emerging from the trees and bushes and everything was being stopped from falling down. There was a beautiful garden pavilion with a flat hat like something from Fatehpur Sikri, and a great square sarai with a huge courtyard, a kind of medieval five-star hotel for travellers and merchants. They watched craftsmen from Rajasthan repair the inside of the dome of one tomb. The plaster ceiling was covered with a pattern of stars like the night sky. Sometimes the four of them would stand on the side of a round curly rimmed hole in the ground, and puzzle over what it was. It looked too big for a well. When it too was excavated the experts found it was a lotus-shaped pond. They filled it with water and put lilies in it.

It was an exciting time, but as things became developed it was no longer possible to have their usual morning explorations. The lost gardens were surrounded by new walls taller than any of them could climb, and so a lot of what had been jungle was lost to them. But Gilly and Mark were happy that there were gardens, and not a road. One day the

work would be complete, and the whole area would be open for everyone to see. Until then wherever the jungle remained, Mishti and Soni would roam, and sometimes they would roam outside the city.

# A MOUNTAIN HOLIDAY

On holidays, Soni and Mishti experimented with longer adventures. Sometimes they roamed in the countryside by fields full of yellow mustard flowers, or green wheat, and past great clumps of sarpat grass, with munias and prinias balancing on their tall flower stems. They watched peacocks and tractors in the fields. Very occasionally they went to places further away too. Once, near Corbett National Park, they met seven of their wild relatives—jackals. The jackals stood looking at Soni and Mishti, and Soni and Mishti stood looking at them. Soni leapt forward to play but Gilly and Mark held her back. They didn't know if the jackals would be friendly. Another time, they stayed in a bungalow in a thick forest on the edge of a dry riverbed. The dogs had to stay inside at night because of leopards. Leopards consider dogs a tasty snack. The dogs had barked a lot during the day, and Gilly listened to the alarm calls of barking deer all night, from very close by. The barking deer must have seen a leopard, and the leopard might well be after the dogs.

One summer it was exceptionally hot. So an expedition to the hills was planned. As the Reva couldn't go far without charging its batteries, they had to take a bigger car. Gilly and the dogs sat in the back—by now Mishti was prepared to look out of the window—and Mark and Kaka sat in the front. They set out eastwards travelling towards the terai, the area at the bottom of the foothills of the Himalaya that would once have been thick jungle but by now was mainly farmland. By mid-afternoon they had reached Tanakpur, where their friends Derek and Susan lived. They were farmers. Irrigation channels ran through their fields, and they had lots of dogs. Soni and Mishti quickly made friends with them, and chased them around barking. They splashed in the irrigation channels while the humans all had tea and cake.

Then everyone went over to see the fish pond. It was long and rectangular, and the water looked muddy but cool. At one end the pipe of a tubewell stuck out over the water. Of course, the dogs and the children of the family couldn't resist going in. Soon someone produced a black-and-white football and Soni and Mishti played swimming fetch. The children would throw the ball and Soni and Mishti would have a swimming race over to it and bring it back, pushing it with their noses. Then Derek decided to turn on the tubewell and the fresh clean water, warm from the ground, whooshed out of the pipe into the pond like a super-powerful shower. Gilly and the children stood under it and felt the weight of the water on their heads. The dogs tried to catch the water in their mouths. When they were all tired they climbed out of the pond. Gilly and the children had a shower and changed their clothes, and the dogs were all washed down and rubbed dry.

Derek brought out food for all the dogs, and the humans sat down to chat and get dinner ready. The next morning they took the mountain road north, to Loharghat, to the most northerly place the dogs had ever been. The road was winding and narrow, with steep drops into a valley on one side. Mishti began to look as if she would rather be at home, and decided to sit on the floor of the car, but Soni had her nose out of the window, her ears flapping in the breeze, and she began to sing with pleasure. They were so high that it wasn't hot any more, just pleasantly warm.

They drove and they drove, stopping just for tea. They entered the wide valley of Champavat, but didn't stop until they finally reached the hilltop settlement of Abbott Mount where they would stay. Abbott Mount was a hill, about 6,500 feet high, covered with forest and dotted with old bungalows. The owners of the bungalow where they had arranged to stay liked dogs. After the normal pats and licks and tail-wags, Mishti and Soni went off to sniff around. Soni found the woodpile kept for the cooking fires. She suddenly appeared round the corner of the house with the most enormous branch in her mouth, eight feet long and so stout that her mouth could hardly grasp it. She looked so comical that everyone burst out laughing. She dropped the log at Kaka's feet. Obviously she wanted to play fetch. Kaka diplomatically put the wood back in the pile and fetched a tennis ball from the car. Then the children of the house played catch with the dogs. After tea the owners set off home, saying they hoped Mark and Gilly and Kaka and the dogs would have a good holiday.

As it grew dark that day they sat on the verandah and gazed at the lights across the valley that merged into the millions of stars in the night sky. A cool breeze made them shiver a little. It was so dark, and so quiet and peaceful.

The next day they set off exploring. Now she was out of the car Mishti was much more enthusiastic. Indeed, she was the team leader. She decided which of the many paths to take and kept zigzagging up and down, her eyes bright as she discovered all the smells and sights. Soni was more reserved. She had not seen nearly as much of the world as her mother, and stuck behind her and close to Mark and Gilly. They passed some of the other bungalows, and came to a flattened area with few trees. Standing on its edge they gazed at the expanse of the high Himalayas, the highest mountain range in the world. All along the horizon were snow peaks. The sun was on their faces, but in the distance they could see clouds.

The next day the clouds sat on Abbot Mount and the trees looked mysterious in the mist. It was chilly and the dogs curled up in their bedding. The day after that more clouds came, this time black and stormy. There was thunder and lightning, and Soni and Mishti cuddled up for comfort, and then it rained and rained and rained. Water hurtled off the tin roof of the house and into the gutters, the lawn looked like a bog, and the flowers in the flowerbeds were battered and miserable. The monsoon was not due yet. This was unseasonal rain. It was difficult to go for walks because of the rain and because the wet weather brought out the leeches.

Small and black and squirmy they would latch on to humans or dogs, and suck their blood, swell and fall off. There was nothing dangerous about leeches, but the wounds they left kept bleeding for a while, and needed to be kept clean and dry to heal. So everyone waited inside for the rain to stop. After two days it did and when the sun came out, the snow peaks of the Himalayas looked bright and clean and close enough to touch. But by then it was time to go home.

The cook, who had kept them warm with his home cooking, told them that he had heard at the local shop that they could not go back the way they had come. The rain hadn't just turned the garden into a bog, mountainsides had fallen and the straight road down to the plains was blocked by landslides, lots of them, and they wouldn't be cleared so quickly. Besides, there could be more rain. Mark and Gilly took out their map, and worked out another way home. It was longer, and it would be a new adventure for all of them.

They packed everything into the car and set off down muddy slippery roads, surprising khalij pheasants with their soft, white crests, and blue whistling thrushes.

Instead of heading due south out of the hills, they were now heading west. Soni and Mishti looked out of the window over ranges of mountains, as the road hugged the contours of the land. Instead of going down steeply, they were staying at about the same height, which made the journey more pleasant for everyone. After the rain the hillsides and broad valleys looked deep green. They stopped for tea to enjoy the view and by lunchtime had reached the road junction that led down southwards to the plains. Even there it was not as horribly hot as it had been. It had rained here too. As they looked behind them they saw more storm clouds gathering, and Kaka drove fast towards Delhi to get there before the road flooded.

It was a long journey and everyone was happy to reach home. HOME. It was a good place. Gilly spread out the dogs bedding in its usual place. The dogs sat in the kitchen doorway, watching Bubbly making chapattis. As soon as everyone had eaten, the dogs curled up and slept very, very deeply—ghore bejke, as they say—not stirring until the next morning. They were exhausted. Quite an adventure it had been.

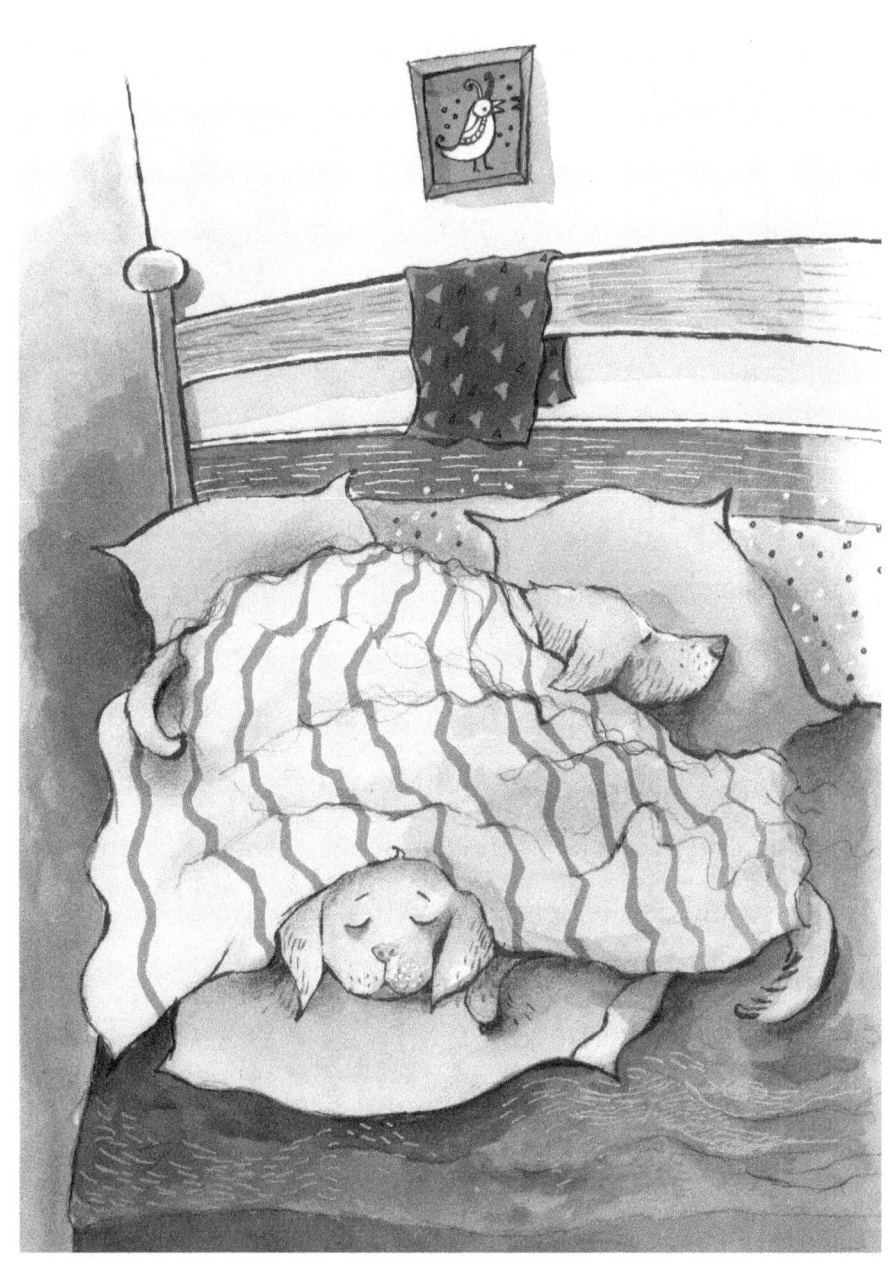

# MISHTI THE MATURE DOG

Mishti and Soni loved their home. They enjoyed the simple pleasures of life like eating fresh chapattis, and playing catch with a rubber hamburger. And they enjoyed friends, especially old friends. Friends who would sit with them on the sofa and tickle their stomachs, friends who would let them lick their ears, friends they could play hide-and-seek with, and friends they would do the fielding for when they played cricket. And especially their they loved their fan club.

They watched Tushi, Nunu and Mana as they grew up and took exams, and still slept in their room, and generally on their bed, whenever they came to stay. Their group of Lodi Gardens friends became even bigger, and they also developed big friends' circles among the street dogs of the jungly places and Nizamuddin. Gilly had been busy getting street dogs near their house sterilized to stop unwanted puppies being born, and then making sure they were up to date with their injections. So these dogs became part of Soni and Mishti's extended family.

Mishti and Soni now had friends as far away as London and Paris. Alex was a special Paris friend. He came to stay with his parents Graham and Roopa when Roopa came home to India every year. He didn't have a sister and so he made Mishti and Soni his sisters. Graham and Roopa planned to take him to see the Taj Mahal in Agra, but when the time came to get up in the morning to catch the train, Alex refused to go. 'I want to stay here with my sisters Mishti and Soni!' he said firmly. And so they didn't go to Agra, and Alex probably had more fun with the dogs than he would have had at the Taj Mahal.

Alex too started to grow up and take exams and Mishti was now a mature lady. She couldn't run quite as fast, or walk so far as she could before, although she approached everything with the same enthusiasm. She spent a lot of time sitting with her front legs crossed looking with great interest as Soni hared up and down after a ball. Her favourite activities were now smelling, and rolling on her back in the grass. She still played mad-wrestling games, but not as much, although she was more of a social butterfly than ever—her tail going tick-tock every time she met an old friend or a new one. And it was always whirlytails for the fan club, and endless barking to greet visitors. As she didn't like driving much, she never went back to Mirzapur to see her birthplace, but Mirzapur came to her. Edward and Sally and Bhagwan Das always came to see her whenever they were in Delhi. And she never forgot a friend.

And then occasionally, she met her doggy family, the puppies that were now all grown up. A special treat was to meet Kim. He had been the smallest puppy, the weakest one who had been born last, but he grew into the biggest tallest Labrador of all. He was much bigger than Soni and much, much bigger than his mother. Sometimes he came to walk in the remaining jungly places with his sister and mother, and sometimes they went to see him in his house with a garden on the edge of Delhi. Soni could be grumpy and growly with her brother, but he was always good-humoured with her. Mishti though loved her son as much as her daughter. She smelt him and wagged her tail and was overwhelmed with joy—her son Kim, an elephant among Labradors.

They could only see him in the summer and in the monsoon because Kim was a dog with a job. In the winter, he travelled down to Kanha National Park in the forests of central India. There he was not just Kim, Mishti's son, he was Kim of Kipling Camp. At Kipling, he had adventures with tigers, leopards and bears. But Kim's adventures are another story, and perhaps we should leave this one with the three of them sitting on the grass in the sunshine, very comfortable and warm, with their favourite humans around them, and secure in the knowledge that dinner time was near.